Hola! I am !
DORA

This is my friend .
BOOTS

This is my puppy, .
PERRITO

We are going to a twin !
PARTY

is excited.

PERRITO

 has a twin.

PERRITO

's twin will be at the .

PERRITO   PARTY

We need to show us the

way to the party.

Look!

has a twin sister!

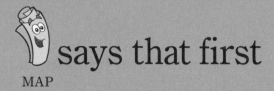 says that first

we must go to the

DOUBLE DOGHOUSE

MAP

and then over the .

TWIN MOUNTAINS

At the  we see a puppy.

DOUBLE DOGHOUSE

He is stuck inside!

BOOTS will try to open the . DOOR

The DOOR does not open.

In English we say "open."

In Spanish we say "abre."

 says "Abre!"

BOOTS

The  opens.
DOOR

The puppy is free.

The puppy has a twin!

Off we go to the  TWIN MOUNTAINS .

The TWIN MOUNTAINS look too steep

to climb.

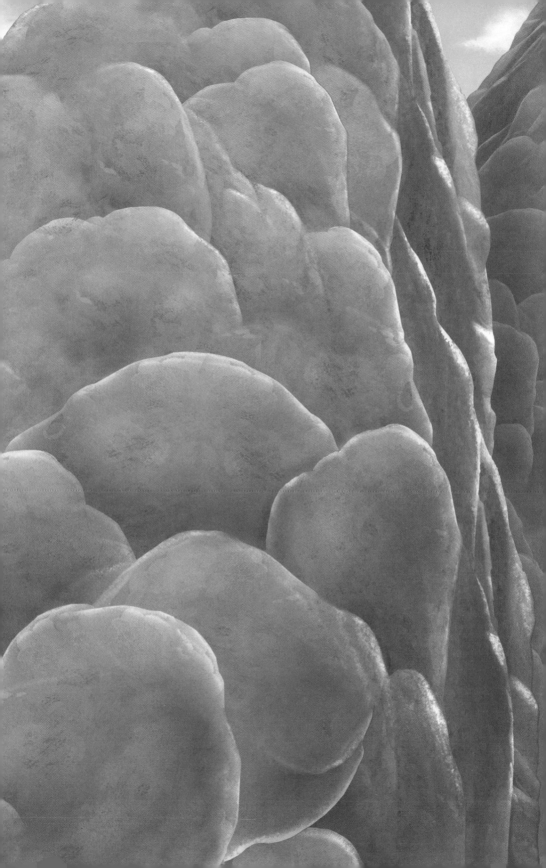

Look! Here come our friends  and !

JOHAN   FRANZ

They have a ⬤ and 🎒🎒.

ROPE   HARNESSES

The  and  can help us!

ROPE   HARNESSES

We all grab the  and .
ROPE   HARNESSES

Up, up, up we climb.

At the top we see a  .
SLIDE

Down we go.

We are almost at the .
PARTY

But 🐶 is tired.
PERRITO

He needs an energy 🦴.
BISCUIT

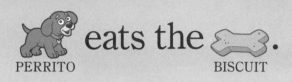 eats the .

PERRITO   BISCUIT

Now he is ready!

Off we go to the  .

PARTY

I see my  ! But  cannot find his twin.

We need to match up

all the twins.

Will you help us?

It worked!  found

PERRITO

his twin brother.

Oh, no! We see 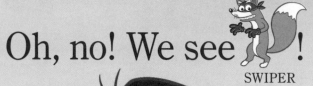!

SWIPER

Is he trying to swipe that ? DOG TOY

Oh!  did not come SWIPER

to swipe something.

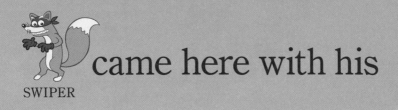 came here with his

own puppy! And that

puppy is 's twin!

SWIPER

PERRITO